This book is
your passport
into time.

Can you survive
in the
Age of Dinosaurs?
Turn the page
to find out.

Bantam Books in the Time Machine Series

#1 SECRET OF THE KNIGHTS
Jim Gasperini/illustrated by Richard Hescox

#2 SEARCH FOR DINOSAURS
David Bischoff/illustrated by Doug Henderson
and Alex Nino

TIME MACHINE 2

Search for Dinosaurs

by David Bischoff
illustrated by Doug Henderson
and Alex Nino

A Byron Preiss Book

BANTAM BOOKS
TORONTO · NEW YORK · LONDON · SYDNEY

RL 4, IL age 10 and up

SEARCH FOR DINOSAURS
A Bantam Book/February 1984

Special thanks to Judy Gitenstein, Ann Weil, Ron Buehl, Anne
Greenberg, Nancy Pines, David Harris, and Lucy Salvino.

Book design by Alex Jay.
Cover painting by William Stout.
Cover design by Alex Jay.
Mechanicals by Susan Leung and Studio J.
Jim Gasperini, Associate Editor.

"Time Machine" is a trademark of Byron
Preiss Visual Publications, Inc.

ISBN 0-553-23602-4

Published simultaneously in the United States and Canada

Bantam Books are published by Bantam Books, Inc. Its trademark
consisting of the words "Bantam Books" and the portrayal of a
rooster, is Registered in U.S. Patent and Trademark Office and in
other countries. Marca Registrada, Bantam Books, Inc., 666 Fifth
Avenue, New York, New York 10103.

PRINTED IN THE UNITED STATES OF AMERICA

0 9 8 7 6 5 4 3 2 1

ATTENTION TIME TRAVELER!

This book is your time machine. Do not read it through from beginning to end. In a moment you will receive a mission, a special task that will take you to another time period. As you face the dangers of history, the Time Machine often will give you options of where to go or what to do.

This book also contains a Data Bank to tell you about the age you are going to visit. You can use this Data Bank to help you make your choices. Or you can take your chances without reading it. It is up to you to decide.

In the back of this book is a Data File. It contains hints to help you if you are not sure what choice to make. The following symbol appears next to any choices for which there is a hint in the Data File.

To complete your mission as quickly as possible, you may wish to use the Data Bank and the Data File together.

There is one correct end to this Time Machine mission. You must reach it or risk being stranded in time!

THE FOUR RULES OF TIME TRAVEL

As you begin your mission, you must observe the following rules. Time Travelers who do not follow these rules risk being stranded in time.

1. You must not kill any person or animal.

2. You must not try to change history. Do not leave anything from the future in the past.

3. You must not take anybody when you jump in time. Avoid disappearing in a way that scares people or makes them suspicious.

4. You must follow instructions given to you by the Time Machine. You must choose from the options given to you by the Time Machine.

YOUR MISSION

Your mission is to travel back to the Meso-zoic Era (the Age of Dinosaurs) and track down a small creature called *archaeopteryx* (ark-ee-OP-ter-ix).

Scientists believe that archaeopteryx may have been the first *bird*. According to fossils that have been found, archaeopteryx had many bones like birds and also like those of small dinosaurs called *coelurosaurs*. In addition, archaeopteryx had feathers, just like birds.

If birds evolved from archaeopteryx, and archaeopteryx evolved from coelurosaurs, then birds may be the living descendants of the dinosaurs!

You must observe archaeopteryx in its own time period and photograph it. Completion of this mission will help confirm once and for all whether birds are indeed descended from the dinosaurs!

 To activate the Time Machine, turn the page.

TIME TRAVEL ACTIVATED.
Stand by for Equipment.

EQUIPMENT

To begin your mission in the Mesozoic Era, you will have special camping and exploring equipment. This includes: backpack, camping stove, inflatable raft, machete (a broad-blade knife), compass, water bottle, hiking boots, first-aid equipment, tent, camera (for photographing archaeopteryx), binoculars, stun gun with tranquilizer darts, waterproof matches, sleeping bag, eating utensils, flashlight, lamp, rope and food. As a precaution, you also will have an extra pack of equipment.

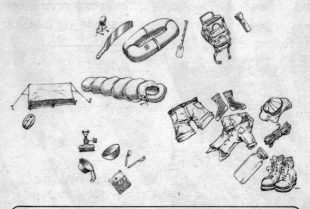

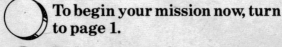

To begin your mission now, turn to page 1.

To learn more about the time to which you will be traveling, turn to the next page.

DATA BANK

Over 205 million years ago, the first dinosaur appeared on the Earth. The last dinosaur died out approximately 63 million years ago. For 140 million years these fantastic creatures walked the Earth.

When the earliest dinosaurs appeared, the continents were linked together. This was the *Triassic Period*. Over the two time periods that followed, the *Jurassic* and the *Cretaceous*, the continents broke apart and slowly formed the shapes we are familiar with today.

Earth during the Jurassic Period

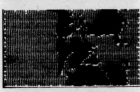

Earth during the Cretaceous Period

Earth during the Quaternary Period (Today)

Over 340 different types of dinosaurs traveled across these changing continents. Some were big, some were small, and some were not much bigger than birds. These smaller dinosaurs included the *coelurosaurs,* from which the target of your mission, the *archaeopteryx,* evolved. Like coelurosaurs, archaeopteryx ate insects and made its home in the forest. Unlike coelurosaurs, its body was covered with feathers!

On the following pages, you will be told about some of the most important dinosaurs of the three periods of the Mesozoic Era, when all dinosaurs lived. Study these pictures carefully; they will tell you which dinosaurs lived in which period, and also about the terrain.

It is important to remember that for prehistoric times, 140 million years ago is *further back* in time than 63 million years ago. You can check the time-line for more examples.

Million Years B.C.	TIMELINE	
570+		
Pre-Cambrian	Early life on Earth	
500+		
Cambrian		
430+		
Ordovician		
395+		
Silurian	First land plants	
345+		
Devonian	First amphibians	
280+		
Permian	Modern insects appear	
225+		
Triassic	First dinosaurs First mammals	
195+		
Jurassic	Middle dinosaurs	
135+		
Cretaceous	First flowering plants Last dinosaurs	
65+		
Tertiary	Hoofed mammals and apes appear	
2+		
Quaternary	Age of man	

the Age of Dinosaurs

The Triassic Period
225–195 million B.C.

A **Kuehnosaurus**—a gliding reptile (not a dinosaur)

B **Dimetrodon**—a tall-spined reptile (not a dinosaur)

C **Plateosaur**—one of the first plant-eating dinosaurs

D **Thrinaxodon**⎤—furry, mammallike
reptiles, ancestors of
E **Cynognathus**⎦dinosaurs and mammals

The Jurassic Period
195–135 million B.C.

A **Camarasaur**—a plant-eating dinosaur from the sauropod (lizard-hipped) family

B **Diplodocus**—one of the longest dinosaurs, also a sauropod

C **Stegosaur**—a plant-eating dinosaur with plates on its back

D **Allosaur**—a huge-jawed meateater

E **Coelurosaur**—a speedy insect-and-meat-eating dinosaur

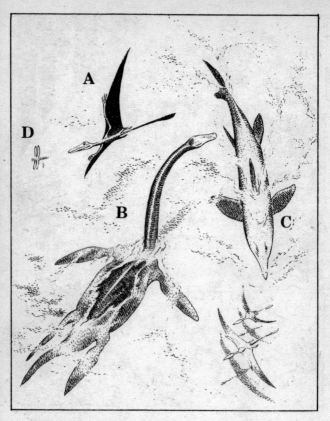

The Jurassic Period (continued)
195–135 million B.C.

A **Pterosaur**—a flying reptile, not a dinosaur
and not a close relative of archaeopteryx

B **Plesiosaur**—sea-dwelling creatures related
to the dinosaurs

C **Ichthyosaur**—sea-dwelling creatures
related to the dinosaurs

D **Dragonfly**—larger than the modern-day
dragonfly, very common throughout the
Mesozoic Era

The Cretaceous Period
135–63 million B.C.

A **Pachycephalosaur**—a dome-skull dinosaur
B **Brachylophosaur**—a duck-billed, plant-eating dinosaur of the hadrosaur family
C **Tyrannosaurus**—a 39-foot-high meat-eating dinosaur
D **Flowering bushes**—these plants first appeared in this period

The Cretaceous Period (continued)
135–63 million B.C.

A   **Pterandon**—a flying reptile, not a dinosaur
B   **Triceratops**—plant-eating horned dinosaur
C   **Ankylosaur**—A plant-eating armored dinosaur with a club tail
D   **Deinonychus**—a meat-eating dinosaur with claws on its fingers and toes
E   **Flowering bushes**—these plants first appeared in this period

For the first part of your mission, you must figure out in what time period archaeopteryx lived: the Triassic, the Jurassic, or the Cretaceous.

For the second part of your mission you must figure out *where* in that time period archaeoptryx lived. Then you must find it and take its photograph.

Be careful. As you are about to see, the Age of Dinosaurs was filled with plant-eating giants such as *brontosaurus,* meat-eating giants such as *tyrannosaurus* and some of the most amazing creatures ever to walk the Earth.

DATA BANK COMPLETED. TURN THE PAGE TO BEGIN YOUR MISSION.

 Don't forget, when you see this symbol, you can check the Data File in the back of the book for a hint.

ou land knee-deep in warm swamp water.

It's hot here in the Mesozoic Era. And noisy! Strange sounds come from every direction through the thick, green jungle. As you step forward, you feel something ripple in the water beneath you. A gigantic snake passes right through your legs.

A shadow blocks the sunlight from behind you. Coming through the trees, towering fifteen feet in the air, is a living, breathing dinosaur! Its huge mouth reaches up to yank a long vine dangling from a tree. You recognize it from the picture in your Data Bank: it's a *hadrosaur*.

Six other hadrosaurs sit in the swamp behind this one. They all have strange-looking knobs on their heads, and they're all eating the same green vines.

You're standing in the middle of a dinosaur breakfast bowl!

The closest hadrosaur twists its neck so its long bumpy snout is only inches from you. It snorts as it smells a human being for the first time. Then it sits up on its hind legs and bleats a sound into the air. The rest of the herd turns and shuffles in your direction. The first one turns, to look for more food, swinging its long, thick tail.

WHAM! It hits you. You fly through the air, smash into the leathery side of another dinosaur, and slide back into the muck.

"Help!" you shout. But there's no one on the entire planet who understands what you're saying.

A shadow appears behind you. Looking down at you is one of the hadrosaurs.

Its huge jaw opens as it reaches down and . . . clamps its teeth on your green backpack.

Of course! It thinks the *green* backpack is a juicy plant. Good thing it's a plant eater, so its teeth are flat, not sharp.

The hadrosaur pulls you right out of the mud. Soon you're dangling from your pack straps, ten feet off the ground!

From this high up, you can see a field, mountains in the distance, and other dinosaurs. It's a nice view, but not if you fall. The straps on your backpack are starting to come loose.

"Let me go!" you shout. You squirm around and hit the dinosaur on the nose.

It blinks and opens its mouth.

FWAP! You fall on the edge of the swamp but not back into the mud.

Now it's time to begin your search for the archaeopteryx.

WHOCK! WHOCK!

You hear a strange noise in the distance. It's not like any of the sounds you've been hearing. It sounds like pieces of wood being smacked together.

WHOCK!

What could it be?

You decide to investigate.

 Stay in this time. Follow the sound to page 11.

You're waist-deep in a shallow sea. In the distance is a shoreline. Fish swim around your legs as you wade toward it. But on land you see no creatures—not even insects.

There isn't even much plant life on the land. It's almost like a desert.

You feel light-headed. You can't stand up! And you can hardly breathe.

Maybe there's not enough *good* air! Green plants give off oxygen. Over millions of years, they produced enough oxygen so animals could breathe the air.

But you don't see any animals here. Maybe that's because you've gone *so far back in time* that the air is unbreathable! The plants haven't produced enough oxygen yet.

Looks like you made a big error!

You're about to pass out. You've got to jump in time, jump to anywhere you can breathe!

 Turn to page 13.

6

ou land in a clump
of bushes.

A hundred yards away, a creature
bounds along. It looks like an overgrown
kangaroo with a lizard's head.

Well, better get to your feet and—
Bam!

Something hit you! You strike the
ground and roll in a tangle of leaves and
stems. Your supplies spill out of your
backpack. Don't these dinosaurs know
any manners?

You look up. Staring down at you is a
large head with big black eyes and a blunt
snout. A sour fragrance like rotting
plants wafts from its mouth. A fern is
stuck in its flat teeth.

It steps forward and opens its mouth. If
it wants to eat you, you'd better defend
yourself!

 **Let this monster have it with
your stun gun on page 62.**

 **Just try to get out of its way
on page 52.**

You're standing by a stream running through a grassy field. On the other side you can see a big nest filled with eggs. You decide to take a closer look.

First you have to cross the stream. Near you is a big log, nearly thirty feet long. You hop on and balance on the rough bark.

You're halfway across the stream when the log seems to twist. You look down between your feet.

This log has *eyes*! The front of the log opens up and becomes a huge, pink jaw. Bright white teeth gleam in the sunlight.

You're riding a giant crocodile—the biggest you've ever seen! The crocodile slips lower in the water to twist around and snap at you. You jump into the water and swim for your life.

The giant jaws just miss you as you scramble up on shore.

You dry off and find the nest in the tall grass. You pick up an egg to examine it. It

is big, the color of sand, and about twice the size of your hand.

Suddenly, something hits you from behind. Squawks of rage fill the air.

A giant bird, with a fat, feathered body attached to long, powerful legs, lunges at you and kicks you away from the nest with its legs. You hold up your backpack as a shield.

The bird won't give up! It leaps at you, kicking you in the stomach. Good thing archaeopteryx isn't as big and dangerous as this bird.

Time to get out of here! But which way—backward or forward?

 Jump twenty million years back. Turn to page 27.

 Jump twenty million years ahead. Turn to page 17.

s you head away from the swamp, the whocking sound gets louder.

The first thing you need to do is to stash your extra supplies. If you ever lose your equipment, you can jump back here for spares, instead of going all the way back to the twentieth century. You find some rocks and hide everything carefully.

A few yards ahead of you, a fifteen-foot-long dinosaur is pacing back and forth. It has a strange bowling-ball hump on the top of its head. It's a *pachycephalosaur*. You turn to get away from him, but there's another one behind you.

The pachycephalosaurs lower their heads, so that their dome-tops are pointed toward each other. You dive into thick plants for cover just as they charge.

WHOCK! The two dome-head skulls hit. *That's* the sound you've been hearing.

You run to a magnolia tree away from the duel. You notice none of the smaller dinosaurs seems to be doing any of the fighting. Are these the females of the dinosaur herd?

It looks that way. The whole pack of larger dome-heads is getting into the act. Soon you're surrounded by pacing, dueling dinosaurs. WHOCK! You jump out of the way just as two of them smash each other's skulls. "Watch it!" you yell. They don't pay any attention, of course.

Right next to you is a big old male who's not fighting. He's lying low in the shade of the trees, eyes alert, watching the younger ones. He has lumps and scars all over his head. If you jumped on top of him, you might be able to ride to safety.

Or maybe it would be safer to jump back in time.

 If you want to ride the old dinosaur to safety, go on to page 24.

 If you want to escape, jump one year back. Turn to page 27.

You feel numb. Something strange is going on. You feel frozen in time while the ocean, the land, and the light speed up around you!

Day quickly fades into night, then blinks back into day. The sun is a streak in the sky. Entire *years* pass before your eyes.

The small plants around you grow to full size, wither, and disappear, over and over again.

This is incredible—you are watching the process of evolution. The land is covered with plants now. It's a jungle! The jungle grows so fast that it looks like a big green blur.

You begin to slow down. You can see the days pass again. The land beneath your feet grows marshy. You're standing on a sandy, dry place between the sea and a weedy pond. You see insect nests in the trees.

Suddenly there are strange-looking fish in the pond. How did they get there? You see a fish flop across the sand from sea to pond. These must be the first amphibians—the first creatures to dwell on land as well as in the water. That must mean that there's enough oxygen for you to breathe now.

The pond dries up, but the amphibians stay on land. They don't need to be in water anymore. According to your timeline, that must mean you're near the end of the Devonian Period.

Time slows down to normal speed.

You take a deep breath. The air is still a little thin, but it's breathable. It feels *good*!

You begin to sink. The pond is gone, and you're stuck in a soft sandy spot.

You're sinking in quicksand!

You thrash at the sand, kick and push and even try to *swim* in it.

It's up to your chest!

The era of the dinosaurs is far in the future. How far? You're in the late Devonian Period—that would put you about 350 million years B.C. Should you jump 280 million years ahead? 320 million?

The quicksand has all of you but your head!

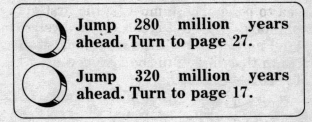

Jump 280 million years ahead. Turn to page 27.

Jump 320 million years ahead. Turn to page 17.

You're standing on a grassy plain. Off in the distance a herd of gazelles is grazing.

With a whoop a group of apes jumps out of the grass. They surround the gazelles and beat them with clubs.

Clubs? They're using tools. These must be primitive men!

You must have gone past the whole Mesozoic Era. Man didn't appear until long after the dinosaurs had vanished.

You walk up to where they're cutting up gazelle meat with knives made of stone. You hold up your hand in a friendly gesture.

"Graagh!" says one, baring his teeth at you. He picks up a heavy club.

Time to get back on the trail of dinosaurs! But how far back in time should you go?

 Jump 50 million years back. Turn to page 8.

 Jump 350 million years back. Turn to page 5.

ou're standing in a large field. You don't see any dinosaurs, but you see movement at the far end of the field. You head in that direction.

Grazing at the banks of a river are what look like horses. But something is odd. The horses are only two feet high! You walk toward them cautiously, trying not to scare them. You uproot a long, soft plant and hold it out for them to nibble. You've gotten so used to everything being *bigger* than usual that it's nice to find something that's *smaller*.

With anxious whinnies, the tiny horses move back a few paces. Then they turn and gallop away, spreading out as they dash. What timid creatures!

GRRRRAGH!

You spin. Slinking toward you is a creature that looks like a wolf. Behind it is a full pack—seven large animals, though they're all a bit thin. They're not exactly wolves—one of them, you can see, has a pouch, like a kangaroo. You can see a small head sticking out of the pouch, riding along on its mother as she hunts for food. The baby grits its teeth and growls, too, imitating the rest of the pack. Hunger glares from their eyes.

This is a type of large mammal you've found here. These pouch-carriers are *marsupials*. By the time man arrived most marsupial mammals had vanished, except in Australia. But none of the mammals got as big as this during the Mesozoic. You must have overshot the Age of Dinosaurs entirely!

But you have *not* overshot the age of danger.

"Go away!" you shout at the wolves. Wolves in the wild are actually timid, you've been told. They're more afraid of the scent of human beings than you should be of them.

The pack splits up. Now each of them slinks toward you from a different direction. They're not afraid of your scent at all! They've never seen a human being. And there are too many to stop with your stun gun.

The lead wolf bounds toward you.

Get out in one piece!

 Jump back to page 1.

A large shadow blots out the sun. A flying creature is dive-bombing you!

You hit the spongy ground. The winged thing misses your head by a few inches and zooms off.

Is this archaeopteryx? It seems about the right size, but you can't see it clearly in the sun. You follow the flying thing along the edge of a lake. It heads for a bunch of reeds.

In midair, it stops.

This thing can't be Archy. A bird couldn't stop like that!

It's an insect. A *huge* dragonfly, with wings as long as your arm! It hovers above the reeds a moment longer, then buzzes across the water.

The water looks cool and clear. You're hot and sweaty. You take off your shoes and dangle your feet in the water. Maybe you could just take a quick dip. . . .

A large green head breaks the surface of the lake. Its snapping jaw is lined with knife-sharp little teeth. With one bite it swallows the two-foot dragonfly, then slides back into the watery depths.

You pull your toes out of the water as fast as you can. You're not going for a swim in *that* lake!

You can hear a thrashing noise in the forest behind you. Something's coming. You put your shoes back on and hide behind a tree.

A furry creature with claws walks out of the forest. It looks like a cross between a lizard and a fox. Fur? That's strange. Mammals have fur. Dinosaurs and reptiles don't.

Another creature appears. It's similar but larger—the size of a dog.

A dog? You thought you were near the beginning of the Age of Dinosaurs. But these things look like mammals. Mammals didn't grow to be as big as these creatures until after the dinosaurs became extinct.

The smaller creature slinks forward and bats away some reeds and leaves with a paw. Within a woven nest lie a batch of eggs. The foxlike thing clamps onto one and begins to suck out its contents.

The doglike creature runs up and jumps on the intruder's back. Those must be *its* eggs! The squabble is a blur of teeth and claws, flying fur and drops of blood.

You wonder if identifying these creatures could tell you what part of the Mesozoic you're in.

You take a close look at the two animals. Do they look like creatures that came after the dinosaurs, or like creatures that came before?

They look at you.

Their question about you seems much simpler: Are you good to eat?

Here they come, drooling and snarling. There are now six of them, eyes bright, claws sharp.

The pack is all around you, closing in!
Take off!

 **Jump 140 million years back.
Turn to page 5.**

 **Jump 10 million years ahead.
Turn to page 6.**

In the shadow of the magnolia tree, you leap up on the back of the old dome-head dinosaur, using the deep cracks in his skin for grips. Soon you're sitting comfortably at the base of his neck, fifteen feet above the fighting.

Maybe from this high up you can look at the trees for signs of an archaeopteryx.

The fighters have churned the ground up so much that it's hard to see through the dust. You see a slightly smaller, younger dome-head come toward you.

Your pachycephalosaur stirs and grumbles. You feel his powerful muscles ripple beneath his hide. The other dueling has stopped. All heads turn your way.

And here you are, sitting on top of this old dome-head. No wonder he was resting, watching in the shade. Those scars all over his head are from fighting all his life. He was waiting until one of the others had enough nerve to challenge him. He's the leader of the herd!

With a growl, the dome-head you're sit-

ting on lurches forward. You grab on tight as he shakes back and forth.

The challenger lowers his head. Your champ lowers *his* head. There's no way to slide off safely.

KA-BOOM! The collision feels like an earthquake, but you hold on. The young dino gets the worst of the clash. You see him wobble away. He crashes to the ground, out cold in a cloud of dust.

The spectators honk. They back away. In another cloud of dust a second young dome-head gallops up toward the champ.

This time you're sure you'll be hurtled into the air at top speed. That is, if you aren't crushed to death!

Time to get out of here.

 Jump 20 million years ahead. Turn to page 8.

It feels like you've been dropped on a giant sponge. The ground is soggy. Giant leaves drip with dew. Is it ever *hot*!

You're standing on a sloping pathway made of crushed plants and flowers. The path runs along the edge of a marsh.

You hear an odd galloping sound. You turn around and see a yellow-and-black-striped dinosaur running in your direction. Two more striped dinosaurs run past the other way. This trampled corridor is like a dinosaur superhighway!

You follow the path until you come to a muddy section. All sorts of tracks cross each other in the mud.

One fresh set of tracks is particularly interesting. The paws that made them seem to end in long, sharp talons. They remind you a bit of bird tracks. They're about the right size to be the tracks of . . . archaeopteryx!

As you follow the tracks, they get farther apart. It's as though the creature had started running! Why? They zig and then zag. You zigzag too. They run around a group of boulders, and you follow.

Suddenly, the tracks stop. If it was an archaeopteryx, maybe it flew off or—

You look up and see a *huge* dinosaur right in front of you. It stands there chewing something, with teeth the length of daggers. Still sticking out from between the teeth is a small dinosaur claw, just about the size of the tracks you've been following. So *that's* why the poor creature was running, and why the tracks disappeared. It was being chased, by a forty-foot-tall meat eater!

You back away, careful not to anger it. When you're a safe distance away, you climb up on top of a rock. It would be nice to get a snapshot of this creature. Before you can get out your camera, though, the rock beneath you starts to move!

You grip the rough top of this walking boulder. It must be an *ankylosaur*, a dinosaur armed with bony covering for protection.

The ankylosaur doesn't seem to like having you on its back. It shakes and heaves, but you are able to hang on.

You wonder if you ought to try another time period. If you're in the Cretaceous, a 130-million-year jump back would show you the Triassic. If you're in the Jurassic,

though, you could jump ahead 60 million years to check out the Cretaceous.

This plated dino must really want to get rid of you. It heads straight toward the giant meat eater, carrying you on its back. The meat-eating dinosaur licks its tongue across its teeth and stares at you. You're the next course of his dinner: "Fresh Time Traveler on Ankylosaur!"

Time to jump in time!

 Jump 60 million years ahead. Turn to page 16.

 Jump 130 million years back. Turn to page 20.

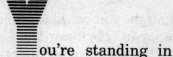ou're standing in a bookstore.

Karl stands beside you, by a rack, holding his Time Machine book.

"We're back in the twentieth century!" you say. "We goofed, Karl. We must have been in 65 million B.C. when we jumped. But why are we in a bookstore?"

A frowning clerk walks up to Karl. "So there you are, young man. Are you going to buy that book or just stand there reading it all day? My goodness! How did you get it so dirty? I'm afraid I'm going to have to ask you to buy it. He looks over at you and your Time Machine book. "And you, too! What have you two been doing? Mud wrestling?"

"Karl!" you exclaim. "You never even bought your Time Machine?"

Karl shrugs guiltily. "Sorry. I thought I'd save some money."

You say goodbye to Karl. The clerk wants you to pay for your book again, although you tell him you've already bought it. To top it off, you're back at square one.

 Return to page 1 and start again!

'm staying here," you tell Karl. "Thanks anyway."

"I really think you should go with me. I know all about dinosaurs!" Karl insists. He seems annoyed.

You tell him no again.

"OK. But you're making a big mistake!"

He disappears. You smile as you finish collecting your bouquet of flowers. Karl said he was jumping 65 million years ahead, to get to the Cretaceous Period. But flowering plants evolved in the Cretaceous Period. So you must already be in the Cretaceous.

Poor Karl. He's traveled too far ahead!

As you walk through the jungle, looking for archaeopteryx, you bump into something.

You stand face-to-face with a mud-brown creature the size of a very large dog. Two horns sprout above its small eyes, another from its snout. It stares at you curiously.

You stare back. Who will move first?

You pet it. Its head is rough and bony. You recognize him now from your data bank: this is a baby *triceratops*. It soon loses interest in you and runs back to a bigger triceratops, which is resting near some boulders. That must be its mother.

Suddenly you hear a loud, angry roar. All the chirping and chattering sounds of the marsh stop. You climb up on the boulders to see what's going on.

A huge form emerges from the bushes by a river bank. Long rows of curved teeth grind hungrily as a *Tyrannosaurus rex* awakens.

You're only fifty feet from the most fearsome creature ever to walk the earth!

T. rex gazes at the mother triceratops backing off behind your boulder.

The baby triceratops emerges from the bushes, trying to follow its mother.

Enraged, the T. rex bounds forward.

The small triceratops turns and gives the tyrannosaur a stab in the shin.

T. rex screeches with pain and outrage. One of his legs kicks out, sending little Horny flying! But the scrappy little dinosaur gets back on its feet and once more attacks the giant T. rex with its horn.

It's very brave but very dumb.

You can't stand to watch such an unequal battle.

You shoot your stun gun. The tranquilizer dart hits the tyrannosaur's leg. It roars again and swings around. It sees you and starts to charge. It's limping, though. The dart is taking effect. You still have five darts left.

The safe thing to do would be to jump in time before T. rex reaches you.

But if you jumped out of this time period, the tyrannosaurus would surely devour brave little Horny! Is there anything you could do to stay here and help it?

 Retreat to the Triassic on page 6.

 Face up to this Mesozoic bully on page 42.

ou test your theory.

You sneak out from among the dimetrodons. One dimetrodon's mouth opens as you pass by. Sharp teeth gleam in the sun. But it's just yawning. You jump over one more tail.

You were right! The dimetrodons just lie there, watching you, waiting for the sun to make them warm enough to feel hungry.

You look at the world around you. The plant life is pretty primitive here: giant ferns, strange bumpy palm trees, a few firs on the hills.

There is one thing you notice about the dimetrodons: they're built low to the ground, with four legs of about equal size. Dinosaurs walked more upright—on big, powerful hind legs, usually, leaving their forelegs free for other things. You must be in the Triassic Period, then, and early in the period, too.

You walk along, scanning the ferns for

flying creatures, when the ground gives way beneath your feet.

A cloud of black flies up out of the ground. You hear an angry buzzing sound.

Wasps! You've broken through the roof of an underground wasp nest. Mesozoic wasps are just like modern ones. They sting! You brush them off as you run, but hundreds swarm after you.

If there were a stream nearby you could hide from them underwater, but the land is very dry in the Triassic. Jump to the future!

 Jump 110 million years ahead. Turn to page 58.

I

t's evening, and it's getting colder.

You set up your tent and sit for a while in front of it. A new moon is rising over the horizon. The earth will look very different in a hundred million years, in the twentieth century A.D., but the moon won't. It will look almost exactly the same.

The sky is full of stars. You check your compass for north and look for the Big Dipper and Little Dipper. Strange— they're not there. You can only see a group of stars that might become the Big Dipper if they moved a little. That must be what will happen. The stars are all moving, but it will take millions of years for them to reach their familiar positions.

You crawl into your sleeping bag, leaving the tent flap open. Falling asleep in your tent, listening to the sounds of the forest, it's easy to imagine you're on a regular camping trip.

An hour later, a rustling noise awakens you.

You grope for your pack, but your hand touches something furry!

You grab the flashlight and flick it on.

You sit staring eye to eye with a whiskered, beady-eyed . . .

Mammal!

The creature blinks, spotlighted against the tent wall. It looks like a mouse or a raccoon. You reach for your boot to scare it off.

You pause, boot in hand, when a spooky thought occurs to you. Man is a mammal. So this creature could be your ancestor! If you hurt the little beast with your boot, you might affect thousands of its descendants. As a result, you might wind up affecting mankind. No wonder the rules of time travel won't let you kill anything!

You shoo the mammal outside and follow it with your flashlight beam. It runs up a tree. You see dozens of eyes reflected in your light beam. A whole family of mammals is watching you.

You zip the tent door all the way up this time, and go back to sleep.

The tweeting of birds awakens you.

You run outside. They're very much like modern birds—in fact, they look like seagulls. You hold out a piece of bread, and one of them nips at your fingers with its teeth.

Teeth?

Modern birds don't have teeth. The archaeopteryx had teeth, like its reptile ancestors, but its descendants gradually lost them as they developed into the birds. You must be getting closer to finding archaeopteryx!

You didn't find him in the Triassic. Here, in the lower Cretaceous, are his early descendants. That means you should be able to find Archy in the period *between* the Triassic and the Cretaceous. You're almost there!

 Jump to the Jurassic. Turn to page 70.

 Jump to the Tertiary. Turn to page 16.

You raise your stun gun. If shooting the T. rex in the leg made it limp, maybe shooting it in the head will put it to sleep!

Ka-bam!

The dart sticks in the creature's neck. It pulls the dart out with one of its small forearms and pops it into its mouth.

You shoot another dart. Now you have three left. The giant takes a step toward you, then another. It twitches its head, looking puzzled. This is it! The giant totters—and drops.

When you're sure it's asleep, you go the long way around the body to find little Horny. The young triceratops huddles by a rock, whimpering. One leg looks like it's broken. What can you do?

You take out one of your darts. "Come on, little guy. This will ease the pain." The triceratops moves back, wide-eyed. You step forward and quickly prick its leg with the dart, just above the break.

You find a pair of sticks in the brush,

and splint the leg with a bit of rope from your tent. This isn't just first aid, you think. This is the *very first* first aid!

You and your new friend follow the beaten-down dinosaur paths. Then little triceratops stops and makes a noise like a bark. It walks up a side path, then back, looking at you.

It wants you to follow!

You follow it into a flat, trampled spot in the middle of a thicket. Five other little triceratopses run up and sniff little Horny's bandaged leg.

This must be the triceratopses' home.

You feel the ground shaking. A gigantic, horned face appears. It's the triceratopses' parent. It snorts and eyes you warily. The young ones all jump around it, making growly bleating noises. You go up to it slowly, so it won't be afraid.

Yuk! Just as you approach, the big triceratops throws up all over the ground! Is it sick?

What are the young triceratopses doing? They scramble over to the mass of half-chewed vegetation and begin to *eat* it.

This must be their supper. It makes sense: When the big triceratops brings home food for the little ones, where else can it carry it but in its stomach? She doesn't have any hands.

You feel the ground rumble beneath your feet. Is another triceratops coming?

The rumbling gets louder. Soon everything is shaking, including you!

You're almost knocked to the ground. Over the tops of the surrounding bushes, you see something fiery red. The nearest mountain, a mile away, is an erupting volcano! Fireworks slash the sky.

With surprising speed, triceratops and her children abandon their home.

You can do the same thing. But maybe this eruption isn't as bad as it looks. It might be fun to watch a volcano up close!

 Watch the volcano on page 51.

 Jump back in time. Turn to page 60.

The flying lizard creature disappears in the forest.

You follow, whipping past branches and vines. If this is archaeopteryx, your search is over! You hear a squawking from the shadows just ahead of you.

You smash into something. Gummy strands stick to your clothes, your arms, your legs. You're trapped in some kind of web!

You're not the only one struggling here. The flying lizard is stuck, too. You look at it closely.

No, it can't be archaeopteryx. It doesn't have feathers. It's just a lizard with wings, which can glide from tree to tree. It was in the Data Bank: a *kuehnosaurus*. Which means you must be in the Triassic Period.

It's time to get out of here. You reach back for your knife, buried somewhere in your pack.

A blob of black emerges from the shadows. Here comes the biggest spider you've ever seen! On odd-angled legs, it navigates the tricky course of its tilted web. The sunlight flashes on a cluster of eyes. A claw in its mouth moves back and forth. It wobbles up to the flying lizard and darts in.

The lizard jerks around, then stops, paralyzed. The spider wraps the lizard up with webbing it spins from its tail.

You're next!

You find your knife and quickly tear through the web, but you keep getting stuck on the thick gummy strands.

Too late! The spider sits right above you. A bit of the web-silk drags behind it. The mouth beneath the eye cluster pinches in and out.

Get out of here! Anywhere!

A hairy leg touches your ear. . . .

 Jump 180 million years ahead. Turn to page 16.

t's cold here. You're shivering.

The sun is high in the sky, but the air is dark gray. Why?

It could be soot from volcanoes. Or something bigger—like the asteroid—may have kicked up a huge amount of dirt when it hit the earth. Whatever it is, it sure blocks the sunlight.

You look around. Trees have been knocked down. The land is barren. It's a wasteland.

Flocks of birds peck away at tree trunks, looking for insects. They hop about quickly, while the few small reptiles you see move slowly and painfully. The birds have a warm covering of feathers. The reptiles don't. Maybe they're too cold to move any faster.

A roar fills the air. There's a tyrannosaur behind you! You've learned how to deal with this monster: get out of its way! You hide behind a fallen tree.

The tyrannosaur doesn't see you. A sad-

sounding growl stirs in its throat. It's thin and looks like it could use a meal. It makes a few swipes at the birds, but its heart doesn't seem to be in it.

You look around to make sure there isn't another tyrannosaur sneaking up behind you. As far as you can see, there aren't any dinosaurs at all.

Maybe Tyrannosaurus rex is *lonely*.

You shiver. Is this the end of the Age of Dinosaurs? Without enough sunlight, the plants are dying out. Fewer plants means fewer plant-eating dinosaurs. And if the cold and lack of food kill off the plant eaters, the meat-eating dinosaurs will die, too.

Poor T. rex! Nasty as he is, you feel sorry for him as he slouches off into the gloom.

You've already passed the time for archeopteryx. You must be in the upper (later) part of the Cretaceous. Should you jump back 50 million years to the lower (earlier) part of the Cretaceous? Or further back, 120 million years, to investigate the Triassic?

Jump 50 million years back to the lower Cretaceous? Turn to page 38.

Jump 120 million years back to the Triassic? Turn to page 6.

he volcano erupts before your eyes.

It's exciting to watch Mother Earth's own "rock show," complete with lights and special effects. Flares spray like exploded rainbows. Lava glows and pours, starting fires where it hits the trees.

Some of the smoke drifts your way. It smells awful.

It sounds like it's raining in the forest around you. Those aren't raindrops, though. They're chunks of rock!

A huge rock comes flying your way. It's twice as big as you are!

You leap out of the way.

The red-hot rock sizzles past you. It's so hot it singes your hair. It digs a crater six feet deep—right where your pack used to be!

Choosing to watch this show was not a good idea. You'd better get out of here!

 Escape the volcano and replace your gear on page 55.

he beast bends toward you. Its mouth opens so wide that you can see the back of its throat. But then it grabs a bunch of leaves from the bush you're sitting in.

You were right not to shoot it. This is a herbivore. It eats plants, not Time Travelers.

Still, it might see a tasty bush behind you, get excited, and accidentally trample you on its way to the picnic. You gather up your supplies and drag them to safety.

Just then you hear something drop down from a branch above you. You jump back so it won't hit you—but it spreads wings, and coasts across to another tree. It looks like a lizard with wings—is it an archaeopteryx? Or something more primitive? Should you follow it, or jump ahead 10 million years, when it might be further evolved?

 Jump 10 million years forward. Turn to page 60.

 Chase the creature into the forest. Turn to page 46.

ou're still on the beach. The sun is higher in the sky. Several hours have passed.

The dimetrodons are walking around now. There's one right next to you. Now its spiny sail is *perpendicular* to the sun, blowing a bit in the breeze. Could the dimetrodon now be using it to cool off?

A mouse-sized creature swims to shore and waddles out on land. It's an amphibian—at home in both sea and land.

The dimetrodon leaps. Two swift bites, and the amphibian is gone.

You back away, wondering about the wisdom of coming here. Early this morning, the dimetrodons could barely move. In the heat of the day, *one* dimetrodon is enough to make this beach a danger zone!

Hunger still shines in the dimetrodon's eyes. It looks at you dreamily. You'd be a nice main course after its small amphibious appetizer!

 Escape 130 million years ahead. Turn to page 6.

ou find your extra supplies right where you left them. You take a quick inventory. Good. Everything is there.

You see a dinosaur twenty feet away, standing in a bed of beautiful multicolored flowers. It's green and fat, with thick legs and a long tail. You don't recognize it from your data bank.

The dinosaur shakes and quivers. Its eyes are watering. Is it angry? Is it going to charge you? You put a dart in the two-foot-long stun rifle and cock the trigger.

As it dips its head back into the flowers, something seems to shake its whole body.

It's *sneezing*!

The flower pollen must be making it sneeze. You snap a picture as it turns and departs. Maybe you've discovered a new species of dinosaur! If you have, you decide you'll call it *sneezosaurus*.

You walk up to the flower bed and pick yourself a bouquet. There are pink and white bushes that look like dogwood and magnolia.

"Hello there!"

You jump. Are you hearing things? That was a *human* voice! You turn

around. Standing a few yards away is a kid. He has a backpack, a camera ... just as you do.

In his hands is a copy of *Search for Dinosaurs.*

"I'm astounded," he says, peering at you. "Do you realize the odds against encountering another Time Traveler in such a wide spread of years? Staggering! By the way, good afternoon. My name is Karl."

You tell him your name.

"Great. Do you know what time period we're in?"

"I usually use my Data Bank to puzzle that matter out."

"No puzzle for me." Karl smiles. "I don't even have to look in *my* Data File. We're in the Jurassic now. The archaeopteryx is millions of years ahead of us, in the Cretaceous.

"I studied up before I left. All we have to do is jump millions of years into the future—about 65 million—and we'll be right where we want to be to get plenty of pictures!"

Do you think Karl is right?

If you do, jump 70 million years ahead with Karl. Turn to page 31.

If you don't, stay where you are on page 32.

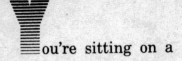

You're sitting on a sand dune.

Behind you is a huge expanse of jungle, before you an endless ocean.

A dip in the sea would be a good way to wash off some of the dirt from your adventures. After all the dangers you've been dodging, it's nice to relax on a safe, peaceful beach.

As night falls, you eat your dinner. You notice a very bright star in the sky.

As you munch on a dried apricot, the star gets bigger.

Soon it becomes a streak of white.

Is it a meteor? No, it's too big. But it's so big! An entire *asteroid* is going to hit the Earth!

It disappears beyond the horizon.

You hear nothing. You can see, though, a geyser of dirt and smoke jetting incredibly high into the air. Anything that big might cause an earthquake or a tidal wave!

You'd better jump ahead a few years to avoid any side effects.

Escape to page 48.

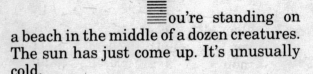

ou're standing on a beach in the middle of a dozen creatures. The sun has just come up. It's unusually cold.

Rising from the backs of these creatures are long spines with webbing in between. You recognize them from your Data Bank: *dimetrodons.*

There's nowhere you can move without stepping within easy snapping distance of those powerful jaws. You get an idea. Maybe they're lined up this way to catch the rays of the sun. Reptiles, most dinosaurs, and dimetrodons like these are all *cold-blooded.* They depend on the sun to warm them up in the morning. When the temperature goes down, they slow down. Should you try and sneak out from between all these waiting jaws, hoping they just don't have enough energy to chase you?

 Sneak past. Turn to page 36.

 Jump a few hours ahead. Turn to page 54.

our tranquilizer dart slams into the huge creature's thick neck.

The creature stops. Its long neck sways. Its tail thumps. It falls, right toward you! You scramble out of the way as it slumps to the ground. You can see your tent flap sticking out from beneath the beast's belly. It fell on your supplies!

You inspect the dinosaur again. A fern is still stuck in its mouth. Its teeth aren't sharp, but flat—good for crushing plants, not cutting meat.

You acted too fast. This animal is a herbivore! It didn't mean to harm you. It was probably just trying to nudge you away from a delicious section of the bush in which you were hiding.

And now you've caused it to crush your gear. Good thing you stashed an extra set.

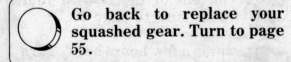

Go back to replace your squashed gear. Turn to page 55.

ou're trudging wearily through a dry, rocky valley. A flying reptile disappears in the distance ahead. You try to keep up with it, but its giant wings are too strong.

You pass a few lizards, but no dinosaurs. You drink a lot of water from your canteen.

You pass through gullies and canyons. You almost stumble over a pile of dinosaur bones. Black clouds quickly fill the sky. Drops of rain begin to spatter in the dust. Where could you find shelter? You're in a dry streambed lined with rocks. You spot a nice, flat, sandy spot, just right for your tent.

You can pitch it now or take another shot at chasing down that flying creature by jumping back a few hours in time.

 Get out of the rain in your tent. Turn to page 78.

 Jump a few hours back. Turn to page 76.

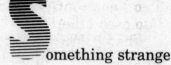

omething strange is going on.

You stop falling in midair—but everything else keeps moving. In fact, it speeds up!

As you hang there, suspended in time, you watch the pterosaurs zip back and forth. Eggs hatch. The young creatures grow to full size and fly off. Several generations speed by: eggs, babies, adults, eggs.

As you watch the generations pass, you can see the pterosaurs changing. Their tails get shorter, and gradually disappear. They lose their teeth, but their beaks grow longer and sharper.

The process of evolution is taking place before your eyes!

The brown vegetation of the flood plain below you turns green, brown, green. Trees spring up, topple over, and turn into soil.

You're going so fast now that years spin past in moments. Now you can see the evolution of the land. A sea rushes in to cover the floodplain. Your cliff is now the edge of a continent.

You go faster, and faster still. Across the ocean, now, you can see another cliff coming your way. The sea drains away. Two huge continents are about to crash into each other!

Wham! When the two continents hit, jagged rocks splinter, higher and higher. You're watching mountains being born!

The movement slows down. You can see individual trees and shrubs again. Slower still, and you're standing once more on the edge of a dry gulch. The Time Machine has found a place in time where it can set you down safely. Where your fall will not hurt you much, where—

Down you go, tumbling. You get a mouthful of dust as you fall. Well, that's not too bad, considering that you've been falling for millions of years.

There's a cliff above you once again. You can see the outline of dark bones in the cliff face. They look familiar—yes! They're the fossilized plates of the stegosaur you saw so very long ago.

Examining the fossil bones are several men—Indians.

"Hello," you say as you approach them. "Pardon me. Could you tell me what year this is?"

The Indians shrug.

"Why are you looking at these bones?" you ask.

One of the Indians looks you over carefully before he replies.

"These are the bones of thunderhorses," he says. "When big storms cross the mountains, you can hear the thunderhorses running. Big fellows, with big bones."

"Are you sure that's what they are?" you say. "Have you ever seen a thunderhorse?"

"No. But what else can they be? We know the bones of antelope. These are not antelope bones. We know the bones of buffalo. These are not buffalo. They are not the bones of any creature we have seen. They are thunderhorse bones."

You think you understand. The Indians have no way of knowing the bones are millions of years old. So they tell a story to explain the existence of these gigantic bones.

A group of horsemen arrives. The Indians point to the fossils. By the look of the horsemen's clothing, you guess that you've arrived sometime in the nineteenth century.

The leader of the group eyes you with suspicion.

"My name is Edward Drinker Cope," he says. "I'm a paleontologist, collecting fossils for the American Museum of Natural History, in New York." He waves at the stegosaur fossils. "I don't know how you got here before we did, but this fossil bed is ours. If you're a spy for my rival, Othniel Marsh, you just tell him—"

"Oh no," you assure him. "I'm just interested in dinosaur bones. But all I see here are bones of stegosaurs and pterosaurs. Where could I find some archaeopteryx bones?"

Cope still seems suspicious. "You mean you've come all the way out to Colorado Territory to steal my stegosaurus bones, and you don't know about the archaeopteryx?"

So you're in Colorado! You must have been watching the birth of the Rocky Mountains on your way here.

"I'm not a spy, Mr. Cope. Please! I know that the archaeopteryx is the link between birds and reptiles. What I don't know is where the first fossils were discovered."

"Not around here, that's for sure." Cope points. "Each dinosaur had a limited territory. The same way you only find lions in Africa, and kangaroos in Australia, the only place archaeopteryx fossils have been found is in Europe. You're on the wrong continent, my friend!"

You thank him and walk off to find a

quiet place to jump in time. You'll go back
140 million years to the Jurassic Period,
but should you head east or west as you
jump there?

 **Should you travel west? Turn
to page 90.**

 **Should you travel east? Turn
to page 81.**

You're standing on the edge of a cliff, looking out over a valley. You step back from the crumbling edge. It's a long way down!

You hear flapping sounds above you. You look up, shielding your eyes from the sun.

Thirty feet above, a flying creature dives through the air. Its wings are stretched tightly over long thin bones, like extra-long bat wings.

Could this be an archaeopteryx?

You get out your camera. It flies toward some cliffs on the other side of the valley.

You walk along the edge of the cliff to a dry streambed. You start to scramble down through the streambed—if that flying creature is an archaeopteryx, you ought to follow it!

Scritch! Scratch! You stop when you hear a strange noise up the streambed behind you.

 Follow the flying creature. Turn to page 63.

 Check out the scratching noise. Turn to page 72.

Scratch! Scritch!

What could be making those sounds? You walk up the streambed to see.

As you turn a corner, you see an enormous dinosaur.

It sits on its side, rolling in the dust. Large, triangular plates grow from its back in two parallel rows. Four sharp horns sprout from its tail. According to your Data Bank, it's a *Stegosaurus*. That means you're definitely in the Jurassic Period.

Uh-oh. Here comes a big monster that looks a lot like Tyrannosaurus rex. It's smaller, though, and faster. Its forelimbs are not as tiny as tyrannosaur's.

An *allosaur*!

Without even a warning roar, the allosaur dashes in to snap at the stegosaur. With astonishing quickness, the plated stegosaur lurches to its feet. It swings its spiked tail at the allosaur, bashing the monster away—toward you!

You run back up the slope.

The world slips from beneath your feet. You're sliding down the cliff! You grab a root just in time.

You're just barely hanging on.

The stegosaur looms above you, blotting out the sun. The allosaur attacks, and the stegosaur loses its balance just like you did. For one brief moment, thousands of pounds of flesh and bone teeter over the edge. Then it falls, just missing you. It slams against the side of the cliff, causing a landslide. When the dust clears, it's gone without a trace.

The allosaur's intended meal has been thoroughly buried. The monster will just have to slink away and find some other prey.

You grope your way up to the cliff edge.

Jaws snap just above your head. Allosaur has prey *right here*. Its powerful hind leg reaches out to help you up—straight into its ugly, sharp-fanged mouth.

You let go your hold, and slide back down to your root again.

There you dangle helplessly.

You venture a look down. Below you is a nest of flying creatures like the one you decided not to follow. They hang upside down, like bats, using the four tiny claw-fingers that sprout from their wings. They don't have any feathers, so they can't be archaeopteryx. They must be pterosaurs.

The rain of stones you've dislodged disturbs them, and they hurl themselves into open air. You made the right choice in deciding not to go after a pterosaur, but now the pterosaurs are after you!

They caw and shriek, ripping at your clothes. They're trying to peck out your eyes!

You lose your grip again.

You're falling!

 Turn to page 64.

You're standing once again at the bottom of the cliff where you first saw the flying reptile. It's earlier, you can tell, because the sun is higher in the sky.

You hear ripping sounds behind you. You walk around a bend in the cliff to investigate.

An awful smell hits your nose. Three of the same big flying creatures perch on top of a dinosaur corpse. They shriek, and flap their wings over your head. You hide behind a rock.

Are these disgusting things archaeopteryx?

You look more closely. They don't have feathers. Their beaks are long. They have talons on the wings. They look just like *pterosaurs*. You spent all that time chasing one of them, and it wasn't archaeopteryx at all!

The wind shifts, and the smell of rotting dinosaur blows your way. It's horrible.

A pterosaur hops into flight. You run up a ravine to get away from the stench and find yourself on top of a familiar cliff.

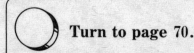

Turn to page 70.

78

As the sky darkens, you set up your tent in the middle of the dry streambed. You finish setting up your shelter for the evening just before it starts pouring.

You throw your gear inside, then jump in.

As you drift off to sleep, though, you feel dampness beneath you. The entire tent floor is soaked!

You tear through the tent flap. A wall of water is surging down the ravine, straight at you! It's a flash flood.

The current grabs you and you struggle through the growing river. You stumble and fall. There goes your tent—and your knapsack. All your supplies sweep past.

Now that was dumb, you think. You set up your tent in a dry streambed, just before the rain filled the stream again!

White water ahead. The stream is about to throw you onto sharp, dangerous rocks!

 Jump back to replace your gear on page 55.

ou steady your-
self against a boulder, determined to con-
tinue your exploration.

As you watch a pair of small dinosaurs
hop across a field, they seem to turn into
four hopping dinos.

How did they do that?

You feel dizzy. The dinosaurs return to
their original number. You've just had an
attack of double vision!

The sun beats down mercilessly.

You sit down in the shade and take a sip
of water. Your face hurts. Maybe it wasn't
such a good idea to stay here. You're
showing the symptoms of sunstroke!
Something is definitely different about
the sun. The dinosaurs around you have
to live with it, but *you* can escape through
time.

If you're getting sick, perhaps you'd better find a doctor! The nearest one is millions of years away.

 **Jump to the Age of Man. Turn
to page** 88.

You're standing on a marshy plain, but everywhere you look there are giant, long-necked dinosaurs—*sauropods*, which lived only in the Jurassic Period.

The ground trembles so hard beneath your feet that you almost fall over. At first you think the sauropods are causing it. But even all these giant feet couldn't make the ground shake that much. It must be an earthquake!

The sauropods panic. A baby bronto nearly runs you down.

All this shaking and running is making you dizzy. You're hot and sweaty and ready to collapse. It's time for a jump in time. But where to? You still don't know if this is prehistoric Europe. If you go ahead to the Age of Man you could ask someone where you are. Then you could jump back again.

Hurry up! The foot of a very scared dinosaur is about to land on you.

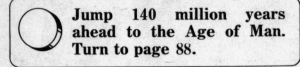

Jump 140 million years ahead to the Age of Man. Turn to page 88.

ou're standing in a sandy river valley, under a hot sun. In the distance you can see a giant animal— some sort of dinosaur, you suppose.

That's strange. You were supposed to be somewhere in the Age of Man.

You walk toward the motionless animal. As you get closer, it looks more and more familiar. It looks like a giant lion, actually—with a *human* head.

It's the Sphinx! You're in the Age of Man, after all. You're in ancient Egypt!

Behind the Sphinx you see a thousand slaves, pulling on a giant block of stone. They're building one of the Great Pyramids.

At least you know where you are. Egypt is close enough to Europe. Maybe there were archaeopteryxes here, too.

Jump 150 million years back to the Jurassic. Turn to page 94.

ou land on the edge of a marsh, right next to a batch of dinosaur eggs. One of the eggs rocks back and forth in the mud. A crack appears in the greenish-gray shell. It's hatching!

One by one, the babies push their way out from their shells. You watch them take their first gulps of air.

One poor baby has two heads! It flops around in confusion, falls over, and dies.

Another one is different, too. Its nostrils are on top of its head, not at the sides.

The baby dinosaurs hobble down to the marsh and drink. Then they wade right in. The one with the funny nose almost disappears. Only its eyes and nostrils show above the pool's surface. A good way to hide, you think. The baby is almost completely covered.

As you watch, the skin on your face feels tingly and warm. You touch your cheek. Ouch! It hurts. You're getting quite a sunburn. You feel a bit light-headed, too.

You've been wandering the Mesozoic for some time now; why is the sun suddenly affecting you? Could there be some sort of extra solar radiation during this part of the Jurassic that's making you dizzy? That might explain why so many of the baby dinosaurs look so strange: powerful rays from the sun could be causing young dinosaurs to be born with *mutations*.

You pull out your compass and check for north. But the needle doesn't spin at all. It doesn't seem to work. What's going on here?

Since there's no way to tell which way is which, you might as well stay in this part of the world. But should you jump in time?

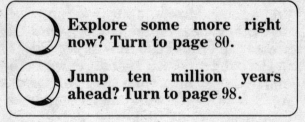

Explore some more right now? Turn to page 80.

Jump ten million years ahead? Turn to page 98.

You're sitting by the side of a cliff, straddling the fossilized leg bone of a brontosaur, which juts from the rock. An old man with a cane hobbles up a path toward you.

"You look weak and weary, young traveler," he says. "You have come to the right place. Beneath you lies your cure!"

"Pardon me?" you say. You hop down from the dinosaur fossil.

"Allow me to aid you, seeker. I am a doctor, here to collect dragon bones. I grind them up into powder, which I sprinkle in tea. This tea has marvelous powers to soothe and heal. You must try some."

No wonder, you think, stories about dragons are told all over the world. Like the Indians, people have been finding dinosaur bones for centuries and trying to imagine the creatures the bones come from.

You take a sip of tea. You feel much better, though you doubt that the ground-up dinosaur bones are responsible. Somehow, the sun doesn't seem as hot here.

"What year is this?" you ask. "Where am I?"

"You must be truly sick," he says with a smile. "It is the seventh year of our blessed emperor, Wu Ti, in the dynasty of Han."

Han Dynasty? You're in China! You're too far east for archaeopteryx, which you now know lived in Jurassic Europe.

"Thank you so much," you say, bowing low to the old man, "but I must go." You walk away, and stop when you're out of sight.

OK. Now you're heading west to find the archaeopteryx in Europe. Should you try the Cretaceous Period again? Or jump back just a short time, staying in the Age of Man, to make sure of where you are?

 Back to the Cretaceous Period. Turn to page 58.

 Back 2000 years. Turn to page 84.

lub! You swallow a mouthful of salt water. What is going on here?

You struggle out of your pack. It sinks immediately. You surge up and gasp fresh air. The sky is clear and blue, the sea is peaceful. There's nothing but water all around you.

You're in the Pacific Ocean, of course. You went *west* from Colorado. Even in the modern age, that might put you in the middle of the ocean. In the Jurassic, when all the continents are still joined together, the Pacific takes up all the rest of the planet!

You're not going to find an archaeopteryx here. You've lost your pack. You take a quick jump back to where you left your supplies and then head west.

Turn to page 81.

You're back in your raft on the river again. But the battling monsters are still shrieking and splashing right next to you! They're so busy tearing each other up they don't notice that they're sinking in the mud!

You watch the fossil-making process begin. The mud will cover the animals and then slowly replace their flesh and bones with stone. That's what Mary Anning will find.

You paddle your raft to a safe-looking landing spot and pack it up. You're about to head off in the forest to search for archaeopteryx when you feel something crawl across your leg.

It's a cockroach, six inches long! Suddenly, you see them all over your pack, crawling on your clothes.

 Escape to the Triassic. Turn to page 60.

 Escape to the Cretaceous. Turn to page 58.

 Brush the insects off and keep searching here. Turn to page 114.

You're standing in a dry Jurassic forest. All the plants are wilted and brown. It looks like it hasn't rained here for months.

A small dinosaur bounds past. Then another two. Where are they coming from?

You smell smoke. In the distance, a tree bursts into flame.

All sorts of dinosaurs run past: big striped ones, little green ones, all afraid of fire. You take a few shots with your camera, hoping the fire has driven archaeopteryx out of hiding.

Dinosaurs running the other way almost knock you down. The fire is behind you, too! You run to your left, then back the other way. The fire is all around you!

The dinosaurs around you honk and bleat. You're trapped with them, on an island of grass in a sea of fire. And that island is quickly shrinking!

There's no way out but to jump in time.

 Jump 30 million years back. Turn to page 85.

You're standing on a pathway in a Jurassic forest, 150 million years B.C. Bushes are stamped flat, trees are knocked over.

You see something wriggle in the middle of the pathway. You look closer.

It's a snake! It isn't moving. You walk parallel to it at a respectful distance.

It seems to get bigger as it goes along. You follow it around a bend in the forest.

It's not a snake at all. It's the tail of a *very* long dinosaur. The trampled path you've been walking along was made by one gigantic sauropod.

You walk alongside the beast. It takes a while before you spot its head atop a long, graceful neck, munching the highest leaves of a tree. This could be *diplodocus*, one of the longest dinosaurs.

This would make a wonderful picture. You lean over and—

A hurtling form slashes past you, ripping your sleeve! Lucky you happened to lean over. If you'd been standing up, it would have gotten you. It looks like an allosaur, but it's only nine feet tall. It's a *coelurosaur*.

Only nine feet? With jaws like that, it

would be dangerous if it were only nine
inches!

Another growl. Right behind you is the
coelurosaur's identical twin. You leap
away as fast as you can toward a sloping
tree with plenty of handholds. You jump
onto the tree and start to climb up, but a
coelurosaur hurls itself after you. Its
teeth clamp into the leg of your pants! The
fabric holds for one agonizing moment before it rips. The coelurosaur falls back on
top of its brother.

You climb as fast as you can, stopping
on a wide branch five feet from the top.
You're missing a few inches of your pants,
but you're not missing any toes. The coelurosaurs wait below.

You take out your compass. The needle
spins around to point north. You decide
not to wait for the coelurosaurs to go
away. Egypt may not be close enough to
Europe anyway; you might jump 10 million years in one direction or another.

 East. Turn to page 81.

 West. Turn to page 70.

 North. Turn to page 92.

You're still standing in a marsh by the edge of a Jurassic lake. This area hasn't changed much in the last ten million years. Sauropods much like the ones you just saw hatching appear here and there in the weeds.

You examine the animals closely. Now they *all* have nostrils on the tops of their heads and longer tails. The one you saw hatching ten million years ago must have been the first. Its descendants survived better than the others. You've witnessed the evolution of a new species! It looks like one of the dinosaurs in your Data Bank—*camarasaurus*.

You don't feel hot or dizzy anymore. You check your compass. It's working again. What could be making the difference? Well, whatever it is, it seems like you made the right choice coming here. But you're still not sure if you've found ancient Europe yet. Perhaps you should make sure by jumping to the Age of Man.

ROAAAR!

You spin around. A gigantic form sways into the clearing. Its red eyes widen at the sight of easy, tender prey.

An allosaur! Again! You're always running into it, or its younger cousin, Tyrannosaurus rex.

Allosaur opens its mouth wide, and a river of drool cascades onto the ground. You leap out of the way as the allosaur charges. You run as fast as you can, hurdling logs and bushes. The allosaur is fast, though, jumping twenty feet with every step. It's catching up to you!

Powerful jaws snap right behind you. You're just not fast enough to get away from him. Better jump in time, before it's too late!

Jump 160 million years ahead. Turn to page 105.

ou're back in a Jurassic forest, 150 million years B.C. It seems strangely familiar. You see a diplodocus off in the distance, and—yes! The coelurosaurs who chased you are still waiting at the bottom of the tree you climbed!

You certainly took a roundabout route to get away from them.

The forest is very thick here, making it hard to see. You climb another tree, one with a good view of the surrounding treetops. You pull out your binoculars and look for signs of archaeopteryx.

You don't see anything. Your branch is wide and comfortable. You haven't had much rest. You put down your binoculars and fall asleep.

You dream you are slowly being covered with a comfortable blanket. It feels nice and snug.

They put another blanket on. It's hot. They're tucking you in so tightly you can't move. "Not so tight," you mutter.

You wake up.

You still can't move.

That wasn't a blanket you felt in your dream. That was a snake! There's a thirty-foot-long snake coiled around you.

The serpent squeezes tighter. Its head hovers, watching you struggle among the pine needles. You pull one arm free and manage to reach your pack. You search for something to use. There! Your fingers close on your knife.

Wait. You can't use it. It's against the rules of time travel to kill anything.

You could jump in time, to escape—perhaps back to the Age of Man, to check out where you are.

But isn't there anything you could do that would let you stay here and search for archaeopteryx?

The snake squeezes tighter. Its tongue flicks at you, as though tasting to see which end of you to start swallowing first!

 Stay here. Turn to page 108.

 Jump to the Age of Man. Turn to page 84.

ou're splashing about in a wide river!

You tread water, holding your pack in front of you. You take out your inflatable raft and pull the tab. You climb aboard the boat, take out your collapsible paddle, and head for shore.

You're still not sure where you are, but you have a pretty good idea. You came south from Jurassic Egypt to get here, thinking that the planet's poles were switched. If you're right, you actually came *north*. Then you might be in the region that will become Europe, where archaeopteryx fossils were found.

You're almost to shore when something hits the boat from underneath, sending you flying. You land back in the raft, fortunately, but it almost tips over.

What was that?

A fin explodes into the air. A long neck shoots up right next to you, shrieking in rage and agony. It's a *plesiosaur*.

There's another creature there, sharp

teeth clamped on the base of the first one's neck: an *ichthyosaur*.

The plesiosaur bats its enemy with its head. The long neck knocks you down as it cranes around to attack. Your raft almost goes over again.

This is not the place to take a boat trip! You could make a short jump in time, to escape, or a long one, to make sure you know where you are.

 Jump 30 million years back, heading south. Turn to page 85.

 Jump 140 million years ahead to the Age of Man. Turn to page 111.

I t's freezing here. White snow and ice lie all around you. In the distance, a ceiling of gray sky stretches over a few mountains.

You see an aluminum shack up ahead. You're *definitely* out of the Mesozoic! A man in a fur-lined parka waves at you.

You start to walk toward him, but you can barely move. The man runs up and grabs you, and drags you inside the hut. You're warm again, but the change is too sudden.

You faint dead away.

Later, you hear a man's voice as you revive. "What's a kid doing out on a glacier dressed like this? I don't know what's going on, Joe."

You open your eyes. You're covered in blankets. The man is in the next room, talking on a radiophone.

"Check all flight patterns anywhere near the South Pole Station," he says. "There must have been a crash."

The South Pole! You must be in Antarctica. But how did you get here?

You pretend to wake up, and rub your eyes.

"Where am I?" you ask. "What year is it?"

The man sits down next to you, shaking his head. "Kid, you're at Coalsack Bluff, Antarctica. It's 1969. Don't try to get up. Just tell me, did your plane crash?"

You shake your head.

"Then what are you doing here?"

"Looking for dinosaurs," you tell him.

The man smiles at you. "Sorry," he says, "you're about 64 million years too late for dinosaurs. But if you're looking for dinosaur *fossils*, you've come to the right place. That's what I'm doing. I'm a paleontologist. Are you here with an expedition, too?"

"No," you reply. "Why are you looking for dinosaur fossils in Antarctica?"

"If we find the same fossils here, under all this ice, that we found in Africa and South America, it will prove that the continents were all linked together once."

"Does anybody else believe that?" you ask.

"There's a lot of evidence for it. Take *paleomagnetism*, for instance. Every few million years the earth's poles switch. North becomes south, south becomes north, nobody knows why. But you can test rocks to see which way the poles were going when the rocks were formed. That helps to show how the continents have moved."

That's interesting. If the poles switch every once in a while, that could explain how you've ended up at the *South* Pole after going *north* from Jurassic Egypt. Nothing was wrong with your compass. It was the *poles* that were upside down!

"Say," you wonder, "do the poles just switch all of a sudden?"

"No. There's a period in between when the magnetic fields disappear entirely, so a compass wouldn't show anything at all. The earth is totally unprotected then from harsh radiation from the sun."

"What would happen to someone walking around then?"

"Well," he grins, "he'd probably get a bad case of sunstroke!"

You hear a burst of static from the radiophone, and a faraway voice calls in. The paleontologist goes out of the room to answer it.

"No crashes reported?" you hear him say. "No other expeditions in the area? But then where could that kid have come from?"

Time to return to the Jurassic, before he comes back to question you! North is north, here in the Age of Man.

Jump 150 million years back to the north. Turn to page 100.

The snake's tongue flickers out, tickling your neck. It squeezes again, making it hard... to... breathe!

You still have one hand free. You dig though your pack for your box of matches. Reptiles, you recently saw, are afraid of fire.

Your hand hits the box. You pull the matches out with great care, and manage to light one. You hold the match right in the snake's face.

Its dark eyes show surprise. Its head snaps back, giving you room to move.

You bring the flame up to the dry needles of the closest branch of the tree. They light easily. You thrust the burning limb into the face of the snake, singing its nose. It hisses and jerks back to get out of the way. Slowly, reluctantly, it slithers off you.

You slip out of its grip and climb a little higher in the tree. You cross over one branch to another tree. You do this several times, putting some distance between you and the coelurosaurs.

You pause to figure out where you are. How did you first arrive in this time peri-

od? You've been hopping back and forth a lot, but you're pretty certain this will someday become Egypt. Archaeopteryx can't be too far away now!

You're about to climb down and hunt when a diplodocus approaches, lurching toward you like a walking skyscraper. You cling to the treetop, as still as possible.

Clouds of insects buzz around its head. The dinosaur's small, dull eyes fix on the needles and cones in your tree. It clamps its massive, flat teeth on a branch just beneath your feet.

The tree sways back and forth as the diplodocus tugs. Your head spins. You can't hang on! You're going to fall!

Escape by jumping ten million years ahead.

 East. Turn to page 81.

 North. Turn to page 92.

 West. Turn to page 63.

 South. Turn to page 102.

ou're sitting on a cliff overlooking the sea. Spring is in the air. Embedded in the cliff below you is a half-exposed fossil.

You hear voices rise from behind some rocks. People emerge.

"Here it is! Over here!" says a young girl. She leads a group of men up the tricky pathway.

"You're a wonder, Mary Anning," puffs a big man carrying a pick. "You must know every stone of these cliffs."

They're English voices. You must be in Britain! You've found Europe, the home of archaeopteryx, at last.

"Hello," you say as they approach.

The girl peers up at you. "Ye'll not be stealing it. It's mine!"

"I'm just looking," you say.

"Bless ye, our Mary," says one of the men, swinging his pick from his shoulder. "Ye've found the bones of creatures that lived before Noah's Flood!"

"This creature has the snout of a dolphin, the teeth of a crocodile, the skull

and chest of a lizard, the paddles of a whale, and the backbone of a fish!" comments another man.

It looks like the bones of an ichthyosaur. It might even be the same one you saw in the lake!

"I don't know what it is," says Mary. "But it was so exciting to find! I'll not be selling this one to tourists. I'm going to hunt for fossils all my life!"

"Ho!" laughs the workman. "Imagine our Mary, gray hair and all, walking the cliffs in 1860."

1860? If Mary will be old in 1860, you must be in the early nineteenth century now. Mary Anning must be one of the first dinosaur fossil hunters.

You study the bones of the ichthyosaur. "I wonder," you say to yourself, "what happened to the plesiosaur?"

And what happened to your raft? You left it in the Jurassic! You're not supposed to leave anything behind when you travel in time. You'll have to go back 140 million years to get it!

You congratulate Mary on her find and say farewell. You turn down the trail to a place where your disappearance won't be noticed.

Jump back to the Jurassic. Turn to page 91.

The roaches crawl all over you. You shake them off and clean them out of your pack.

You may not like insects very much, but *archaeopteryx* loves them! That's what Archy eats.

You've found ancient Europe, where archaeopteryx lived, you're here in the Jurassic, his time period, and now you've discovered a big supply of his favorite meal. You may be able to find archaeopteryx at last!

You sit at the river bank and let your feet dangle in cool water. You watch pterosaurs swoop down to the river, catching fish with their claws.

You lift your camera to take a picture of them, but it slips from your hands into the swift current of the river.

Without your camera, you've no hope of completing your mission! You race down the river bank. The camera floats along in its waterproof case.

A pterosaur swoops down, splashing

into the water. When it emerges, the camera dangles from its claws. The flying reptile soars over you, landing high in a nearby tree.

How are you going to get the camera back?

The pterosaur drops the camera onto the branch beneath it, squawking in frustration. Cameras just aren't very tasty! It dives back toward the river, leaving your camera balanced on the branch, thirty feet above the ground.

You climb the tree carefully, trying not to shake the upper branches. If your camera falls to the ground, it will be smashed.

Finally, you reach the branch. Holding fast with your other hand, you reach out . . .

But your feet slip off! You dangle by one hand. The tree sways back and forth.

You catch another branch with your foot and regain your balance. You grab the camera and rest on the branch.

You look down at the ground far below. You can see a pit in the soft earth a few dozen feet from the river bank. The pit is full of dinosaur eggs. Scurrying down the tree, you make your way to the nest.

Each egg is only a couple of inches high. There are about a dozen of them.

Crack!

A head pops out of one of the eggs. Then another one hatches.

"Awwk! Awkk!" the new arrivals cry. They look like little birds, with wet feathers. No, they really look more like little dinosaurs, with scaly claws and teeth.

Wait a minute. Wet feathers? A little like a dinosaur?

Darkness is gathering quickly. You attach your camera's flash and kneel down close to the nest.

Squawwk!

You look behind you. There, hopping back and forth angrily, is a creature about a foot high. It has feathers. It flaps its wings. There are teeth in its beak.

"Archaeopteryx?" you say. "You're an archaeopteryx!"

It opens its beak to squawk again, its beady eyes flashing. Its feathers seem to bristle. Layers of red and brown cover a thin body, spreading out into a wide tail almost like a beaver tail. You snap its picture.

Archaeopteryx jumps back as your flash goes off. She squawks in anger and confusion. She doesn't want you bothering her young. She dances from leg to leg like a frantic rooster.

You finally have a photograph of archaeopteryx, the first bird! Now all you have to do is get safely back to the present, and you're done.

A shadow falls over your pack. You look

up and see an allosaurus! It sweeps you up with its talons, holding you ten feet high in the air. You could jump in time now, but then you'd be leaving your gear behind. What to do? The allosaurus is opening its huge mouth to stuff you in!

Your camera still dangles from your neck. You bring it up and click. A flash goes off right in allosaurus's face!

Startled, the allosaurus drops you right on your pack. You pick it up quickly and jump to a time when the most dangerous creatures are human beings.

Then again, perhaps it's actually safer back in the Mesozoic!

MISSION COMPLETED

DATA FILE

DATA FILE

About the Contributors

DAVID BISCHOFF is a well-known author of science fiction and fantasy. His novels include *Nightworld, The Day of the Dragonstar,* and *The Selkie* (with Charles Sheffield). He is an active member of the Science Fiction Writers of America and currently resides in Virginia. His latest book is *WarGames,* a novelization of the feature film.

DOUG HENDERSON is a respected illustrator and fine artist whose depictions of the Mesozoic Era have won the admiration of paleontologists and aficionados of natural history art. He has recently completed a children's book with dinosaur expert Jack Horner, and continues to research his favorite subject at the sites of dinosaur digs. He currently resides in Wyoming.

ALEX NINO is an internationally respected illustrator. His work has appeared in such publications as *Metal Hurlant* in France, *Starlog* in America and in hundreds of magazines in his native Philippines. His paintings and illustrations have been published as portfolios, book jackets, and graphic stories. He is also the winner of an Inkpot Award.

CHOOSE YOUR OWN ADVENTURE ®

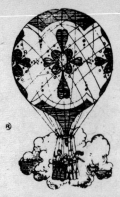

"You'll want all the books in the exciting Choose Your Own Adventure series. Each book takes you through dozens of fantasy adventures—under the sea, in a space colony, into the past—in which *you* are the main character. What happens next in the story depends on the choices *you* make, and *only you* can decide how the story ends!"